SPORTS FOR SPROUTS

BASKETBALL

Tracy Nelson Maurer

www.rourkepublishing.com

© 2011 Rourke Publishing LLC

All rights reserved. No part of this book may be reproduced or utilized in any form or by any means, electronic or mechanical including photocopying, recording, or by any information storage and retrieval system without permission in writing from the publisher.

www.rourkepublishing.com

The author wishes to thank Meredith Nelson and Anders Nelson for their enthusiastic assistance.

Photo credits: All photo's © blue door publishing, except:
Cover © Slavoljub Pantelic, Ginos photos; Title Page © Wendy Nero, Crystal Kirk, Leah-Anne Thompson, vnosokin, Gerville Hall, Rob Marmion; Page 3 © Daniel Bendjy; Page 7 © Diane Uhley; Page 8 © Jorge Pedro Barradas de Casais; Page 16 © Andrew Rich; Page 19 © Linda Hughes; Page 22 © Andrew Rich, Diane Uhley, blue door publishing; Page 23 © Andrew Rich, blue door publishing

Editor: Jeanne Sturm

Cover and page design by Nicola Stratford, Blue Door Publishing

Library of Congress Cataloging-in-Publication Data

Maurer, Tracy, 1965-
 Basketball / Tracy Nelson Maurer.
     p. cm. -- (Sports for sprouts)
 Includes bibliographical references and index.
 ISBN 978-1-61590-235-4 (Hard cover) (alk. paper)
 ISBN 978-1-61590-475-4 (Soft cover)
 1. Basketball--Juvenile literature. [1. Basketball.] I. Title.
 GV885.1.M38 2010
 796.323--dc22
                                              2010009018

Rourke Publishing
Printed in the United States of America, North Mankato, Minnesota
033010
033010LP

www.rourkepublishing.com - rourke@rourkepublishing.com
Post Office Box 643328 Vero Beach, Florida 32964

I play basketball.

A basketball team has five players.

A high **basket** stands at each end of the **court**.

Shooting the basketball through the net earns points.

We try to **block** the other team.

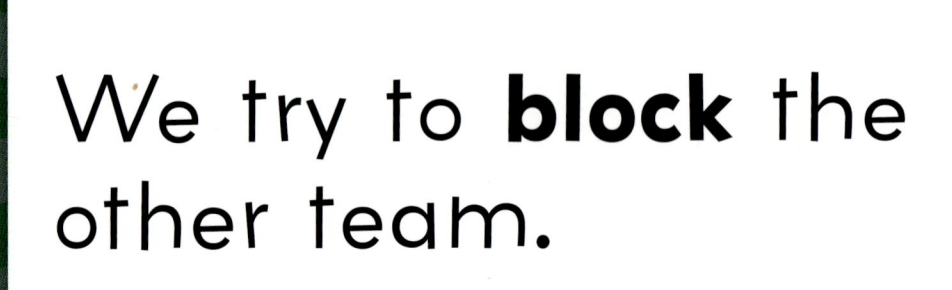

We **dribble** the ball.

We **pass** the ball to our teammates.

We **shoot** the ball at the basket.

Swoosh! The ball drops in for two points.

The team with the most points wins.

Picture Glossary

basket (BASS-kit): A basket has a hoop with a net hanging below it. The hoop is on a backboard that helps players bounce the ball through the net.

block (BLOK): To block, a basketball player might wave his or her arms or catch a pass meant for the opposite team. No pushing allowed!

court (KORT): A court is a rectangle-shaped field, usually covered in wood or paved, with lines on it to show where to play the game. It also has two baskets.

dribble (DRIB-uhl): To dribble, a player bounces the ball with one hand. A player must dribble the ball while walking or running.

pass (PASS): To pass the ball, a player tosses the ball to a teammate.

shoot (SHOOT): To throw the ball to the basketball net. If it goes through the net you score points for your team.

Index

basket 6, 17
block 10
court 6
dribble 13

pass 14
points 9, 18, 21
teammates 14

Websites

www.pecentral.org/websites/kidsites.html
www.nba.com/kids/
www.pbskids.org/kws/sports/basketball.html

About the Author

Tracy Nelson Maurer loves to play with her two children and husband in their neighborhood near Minneapolis, Minnesota. She holds an MFA in Writing for Children & Young Adults from Hamline University, and has written more than 70 books for young readers.

SPORTS FOR SPROUTS

Fit kids are healthy kids, and the Sports for Sprouts books help emergent readers learn about ways to stay active. Each book explains the basic rules, skills, and clothing involved in a sport or activity. The books also emphasize teamwork and good sportsmanship. Full-page color photographs engage young learners and make reading fun.

Books In This Series:
Baseball
Basketball
Bicycle Riding
Cheerleading
Dance
Gymnastics
Karate
Playground Games
Soccer
Swimming

ISBN 978-1-61590-475-4

9 781615 904754

www.rourkepublishing.com